Kevin

Based on
The Railway Series
by the
Rev. W. Awdry

Illustrations by
Robin Davies
and **Jerry Smith**

EGMONT

EGMONT

We bring stories to life

First published in Great Britain in 2017
by Egmont UK Limited
The Yellow Building, 1 Nicholas Road, London W11 4AN

Thomas the Tank Engine & Friends™

CREATED BY BRITT ALLCROFT

HiT entertainment

ISBN 978 1 4052 8572 8
66168/1
Printed in Italy

Written by Emily Stead. Designed by Claire Yeo.
Series designed by Martin Aggett.

FSC
MIX
Paper
FSC® C018306

Egmont is passionate about helping to preserve the world's remaining ancient forests.
We only use paper from legal and sustainable forest sources.

This book is made from paper certified by the Forestry Stewardship Council® (FSC®),
an organisation dedicated to promoting responsible management of forest resources.
For more information on the FSC, please visit www.fsc.org. To learn more about Egmont's
sustainable paper policy, please visit www.egmont.co.uk/ethical

*Kevin the little crane helps
Victor mend engines at the
Steamworks. Kevin may be
clumsy, but he is helpful and
kind. Could he rescue a big
engine in trouble?*

Early one morning at the Steamworks, all was quiet. Then suddenly, **"Peep! Peep! Peep!"** went an engine rushing by.

"Trembling tracks!" cried Kevin. "What was that?"

"That's Spencer's whistle," Victor replied.

Snooty Spencer was visiting from the Mainland. He wanted everyone to know he had arrived.

Victor and Kevin began the day's work. They loved helping broken-down engines get back on track.

Kevin rolled to collect some engine parts, still half-asleep. **CLANG!** went the parts, as they crashed on the floor. Victor shut his eyes.

"Sorry, boss," said Kevin. "It was a slip of the hook!"

Meanwhile, Spencer steamed to Tidmouth Sheds. **"Peep! Peep!** Wake up, lazybones!" he whistled.

Gordon was cross. He didn't like being woken up.

"You need a wash down, Gordon," Spencer teased. "See how shiny my silver paint is!"

This made Gordon even more cross!

Thomas set off for the Steamworks. He needed Victor and Kevin to mend a crack in his funnel.

Spencer steamed after him. "Let's race!" he said.

But Thomas didn't want to race. He wanted to get his funnel fixed, so he could be a Really Useful Engine again.

"Scaredy-engine!" Spencer teased.

Thomas and Spencer arrived at the Steamworks. Kevin was so excited that he rolled straight into a heap of scrap! **CLANG! CRASH!**

"Hello, Spencer!" Kevin smiled. "Do you need a helping hook?"

"No, I do not!" Spencer sneered. "Big engines like me **never** break down."

Kevin wanted to show Spencer how strong he was, but his heavy load slipped from his hook. **CLANG! CRASH! BANG!**

"You clumsy crane! **WHAT A DIN**!" Spencer cried.

"Haven't you got a job somewhere, Spencer?" Victor said sternly.

Spencer was shocked! He steamed away without a word.

Spencer passed Gordon, pulling the Big Express.

"Peep! Peep! How do you like my Express train?" boasted Gordon.

Spencer tried to call back, but his whistle wouldn't work. He had lost his voice from shouting at Kevin!

"He's dreadfully rude!" Gordon said to his Driver.

That night in the Sheds, the engines were talking about how rude Spencer had been that day.

"He should learn some manners," said James.

But Spencer said nothing. The engines thought he was ruder still when he didn't say sorry.

Spencer went to sleep, his wheels full of worry.

The next morning, Spencer still couldn't speak. He couldn't ask Kevin and Victor to mend him, because he had been so rude to Kevin.

He set off to take the Duke and Duchess to the Docks. The track ran behind the Steamworks.

All of a sudden, Spencer stopped with a **splutter**. He had run out of water!

Spencer tried to whistle, but all that came out was a funny muffled sound.

Kevin heard the funny whistle, and rolled outside. He was surprised to find Spencer, broken down.

"Don't worry, Spencer," Kevin said kindly. "We can fix you."

Spencer smiled back at the little crane.

While Spencer's whistle was being mended, Kevin gave him a long drink of water.

"Thank you," said Spencer. "I'm sorry I was rude."

Kevin worked carefully. He tidied trucks and moved metal, without a single clang. Spencer took the Duke and Duchess to their ferry, just in time.

Kevin and Spencer are now good friends. Spencer often visits Kevin, and he **never** shouts.

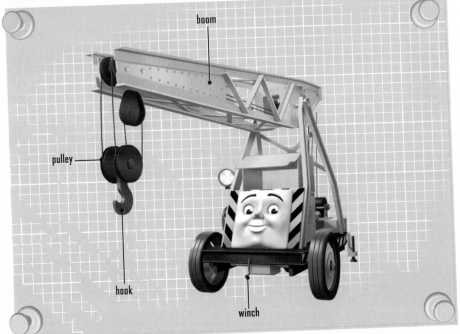

boom

pulley

hook

winch

Kevin's challenge to you

Look back through the pages of this book
and see if you can spot:

hook

moon

pigeon

bucket

donkey